The Loneliest Star

By Robert Gaines

Illustrated by Taras Kostiuk

Anava,
Stay a bright happy star, Enjoy the book
Robert Gaines

ISBN: 0692733388
ISBN-13: 978-0692733387

Special thanks to Christopher Hawke and Traci Hall of CommunityAuthors.com, in Ft. Lauderdale, Florida.

When you look into the sky on a clear night you see it's full of bright twinkling stars. Most of them are very far away.

Once there was a lonely star named Cobby. As stars go, he was very young. He lived in space, far from his friend, another star, Old Stellar. Cobby had no planets, no one spinning and revolving around him, like other stars in the universe. This made him lonely.

Cobby wanted to give light and warmth to planets, like Old Stellar did. Old Stellar was much older than Cobby and didn't always appreciate his good fortune.

"Cobby," Old Stellar cried out, "Why do you want to have planets? When you have planets revolving around you, you encounter living things like people, animals and plants. With the help of your power, they can all be striking and beautiful, but people are rarely satisfied."

Old Stellar gave Cobby a stern look and said, “I hear people complain that it is too cold, too hot, too dry, too wet, too dark and too bright. They want snow, they don’t want snow. They want the sun to shine; they don’t want the sun to shine. I wish I could be alone in the cold darkness just like you. You don’t want planets. That would make you a sun, young Cobby.”

Cobby frowned. “I do want to become a sun. What good is power and energy if it is not put to good use? I have the ability to bring warmth and light to entire worlds. Yet, I’m alone in the cold darkness. Planets need both cold and warmth, rain and sun, light and dark to exist.”

Old Stellar sighed. “What a foolish young star.”

The two of them had other friends like the moons, Gemma and Zempy. They made Cobby smile. Old Stellar saw them as pests, always following him in space.

Gemma warned Old Stellar that gravity was pulling Zempy on an unusual course. He wasn't traveling his normal path. Old Stellar knew Gemma had the ability to see this, but didn't worry too much about it.

It so happens revolving around Old Stellar was a beautiful and lush planet called Ahee.

TAXI
TAXI
SUN AVENU

Those who lived there were happy. They worked hard, played hard and were free. They appreciated their lives and the blessings they were given. To celebrate their good fortune, every year they had a giant, planet-wide, picnic. They played fun games and enjoyed each other's company. This year was special. They had many years of peace and happiness to celebrate. Delicious food was prepared, and the fields and lawns were readied for games to be played by children and adults alike.

As the big day arrived, there was a light blue sky, and the temperature was just right. Excited children and adults swam in the lakes and played catch and tag. Their excitement could be heard throughout the land. Love and compassion were present everywhere.

At midday, it was time for the festive meal. Blankets were spread out on the freshly cut lawns. It was the grandest picnic they ever had.

Just as people were sitting down to enjoy their food, a terrible thing happened. It became totally dark! Even though it was the middle of the day, it looked just like night. It appeared the gala celebration was over.

"Help, what happened?" They looked to the darkening sky and yelled, "Where is Old Stellar?"

Old Stellar was still there. Zempy, while traveling through the sky, accidentally passed between Old Stellar and Ahee which blocked the warmth and light of his rays. This is called an eclipse.

No one on Ahee had ever seen an eclipse. They had seen the moons lit up in the night sky and sometimes they saw them during the day but they never saw a moon black out their sun. Their shouts could be heard far out into space.

Cobby heard their yells and wondered what was wrong. He looked down to planet Ahee to get a better view. “Oh my, it has become dark right in the middle of the day! I must do something to help.”

Cobby was very far away but tried to bring light to those crying in the dark. He wasn’t able to get his rays to travel all the way to Ahee.

It is a fact that if we put our minds to it we can do wonderful things. Sometimes we can do things we never thought possible. Cobby was intent on succeeding. Thinking about his friends, Old Stellar, Gemma, and Zempy, he gathered as much strength as he could.

He strained and strained and strained some more. Finally, gathering enough energy and power, he sent his warmth and light the entire distance to Ahee.

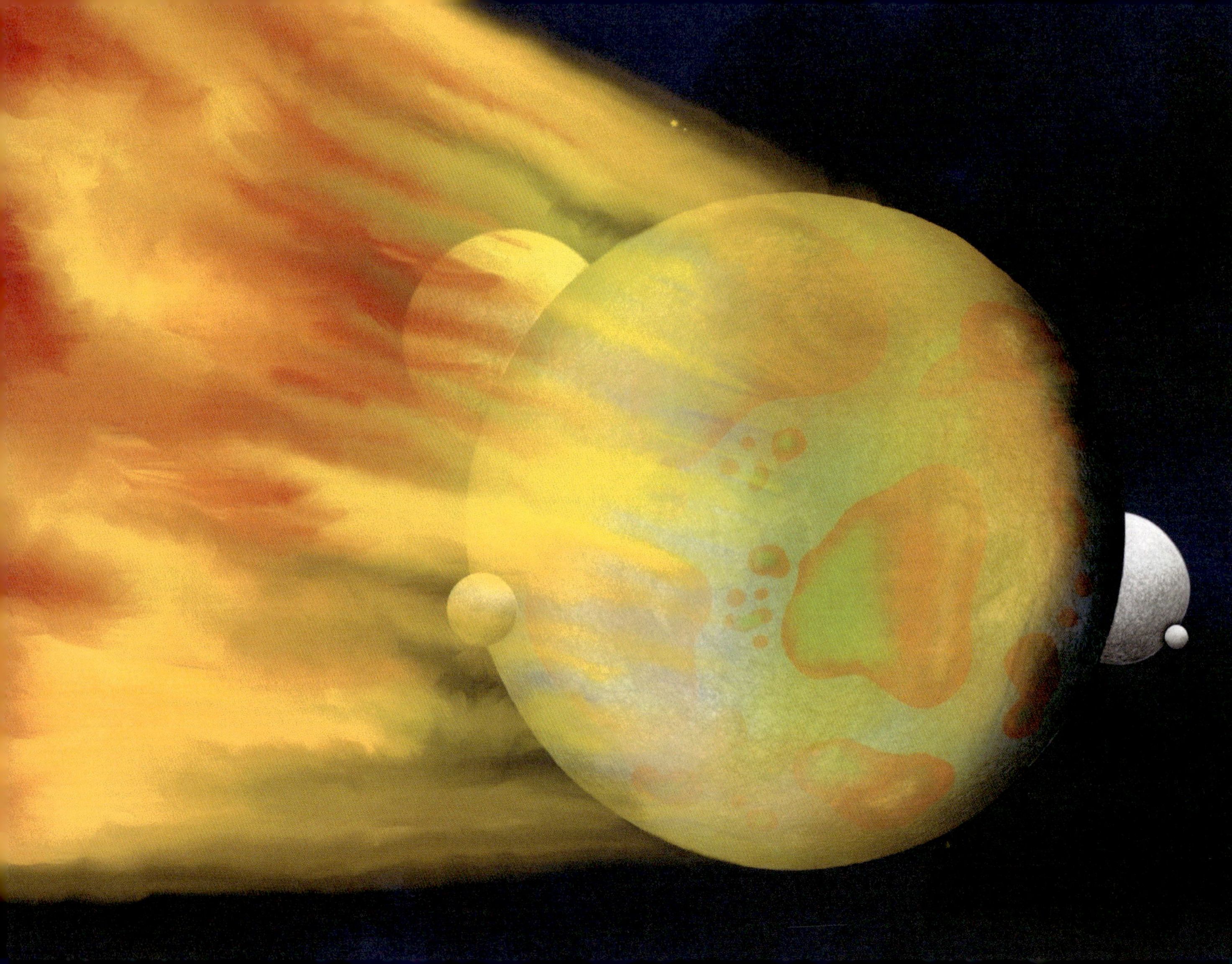

Slowly, the entire planet came back to life. The gala event was saved and the people continued their celebration.

They looked up to the sky.

"Hooray for Cobby!" they yelled. "Thank you. You saved the day."

Cobby was tired but very happy.

The people of Ahee enjoyed the picnic so much they called Cobby a sun. This made him proud.

Cobby realized that even when someone feels alone they can still give light and warmth to others.

He was never lonely again.

About the Author

Robert Gaines lives in South Florida with his cat Kip. The Loneliest Star was born from his own observations of the nighttime sky. Be sure to look for Cobby's next adventure, The Friendliest Star!

Made in the USA
Charleston, SC
20 November 2016